The Very Fairy Princess

by Julie Andrews & Emma Walton Hamilton

Illustrated by

Christine Davenier

LB

Little, Brown and Company

New York   Boston

Hi! I'm Geraldine.

I'm a fairy princess.

You may not believe me, but I can tell you that *I AM.*

I know that I'm a fairy princess because *I* FEEL it inside—
a sparkly feeling of just KNOWING in my heart.
Also, I do EVERYTHING that fairy princesses do.

The first thing I do when I wake up in the morning
is put on my crown.

(Fairy princesses are ALWAYS presentable. You never know
who you might bump into…even on the stairs.)

For breakfast I have Fairy Pancakes, with extra fairy dust on top.
YUM!

(Fairy princesses have very refined taste.)

Then it's time to choose my royal attire for the day.
The BIG decision is which dress to wear: pink and white,
pink and purple, pink and red…or just PINK?

My brother, Stewart, says fairy princesses
don't wear sneakers and don't have scabby knees.
I say sneakers help me practice my flying skills, ESPECIALLY when
we're late for the school bus, and scabs are the price you pay.

(Fairy princesses are very practical.)

My best friend, Delilah, doesn't
believe that I'm a fairy princess.
I say you can be whatever you want to be.
You just have to let your SPARKLE out!

"For instance," I tell her, "YOU sparkle
when you play the trombone."

(Fairy princesses are very supportive.)

Flying is NOT allowed in class.

So at school, I hang my wings up in my cubby.

(Besides, they'd get squished in morning meeting.)

My teacher, Miss Pym, says fairy princesses don't fidget or interrupt.
But how else can you be on the lookout for problems to solve?
Sometimes you HAVE to speak up—like when our class pet,
Houdini the hamster, escapes.

(Fairy princesses know when to take charge.)

My favorite classes are art and music.
That's when I can REALLY let my sparkle out!
I use lots of glitter, sequins, and feathers when I paint. Sometimes there's just not enough space on the wall for all my pictures!

(Fairy princesses like to keep extra gifts on hand
for special occasions—like when Grandma comes to visit.)

All fairy princesses LOVE to sing.
Once in a while I get carried away, and
Mr. Higgenbottom reminds me there's only
room for one conductor in the chorus.

The absolute BEST time of the week is
when I have ballet after school.
I wear my fluffy tutu, and twirl and whirl
and leap—light as a feather!

Occasionally my crown gets in the way,
but I'm working on that.

(Fairy princesses know that practice makes PERFECT.)

Back home, it's time for my fairy snack—pink lemonade
and sugar cookies with extra sprinkles.
(DOUBLE YUM!)

Then it's into the garden I go,
to attend to my royal duties…

like rescuing frogs (you never know
when one might be a PRINCE!),

building little houses
for my fellow fairies,

and exercising my unicorn.

Mom calls me in for my bath.
She says fairy princesses don't have dirty fingernails.
I say it's the price you pay for having so many responsibilities!

I have to remove my crown to shampoo my hair,
but I make one out of BUBBLES just to tide me over.

(Fairy princesses are very creative.)

Stewart says fairy princesses shouldn't watch TV
before they've done their homework.
I say even a fairy princess needs a break,
to keep her sparkle from sagging!

(BESIDES, how else can you keep up with the fairy news of the day?)

Daddy KNOWS I'm a fairy princess.
When he comes home from work, he always says,
"How's my little princess today?"
So that's all right.

Being a fairy princess can be very demanding.
Sometimes it's all I can do to stay awake through dinner.

(Fairy princesses need lots of beauty sleep to RECHARGE their sparkle!)

Daddy carries me up to bed.

Mommy tucks me in.

"Sweet dreams, Gerry," they whisper from the door.
"You'll always be our VERY fairy princess!"